BEAUTIFUL (BROKEN) HEART

BEAUTIFUL (BROKEN) HEART

POEMS BY:

DAVINA FERREIRA

PART I

BREAKING

HEARTBREAK　　　　　　　　　　　A F T E R

HEARTBREAK　AFTER　　　　HEARTBREAK　AFTER

HEARTBREAK　AFTER　HEARTBREAK　　　AFTER　HEARTBREAK　　AFTER

HEARTBREAK　AFTER　HEARTBREAK　AFTER　　HEARTBREAK　AFTER　HEARTBREAK　AFTER

HEARTBREAK　AFTER　HEARTBREAK　AFTER　　HEARTBREAK　AFTER　HEARTBREAK　AFTER

HEARTBREAK　AFTER　HEARTBREAK　AFTER　HEARTBREAK　AFTER　HEARTBREAK　AFTER

HEARTBREAK　AFTER　HEARTBREAK　AFTER　HEARTBREAK　AFTER　HEARTBREAK　AFTER　HEARTBREAK

AFTER　HEARTBREAK　AFTER　HEARTBREAK　AFTER　HEARTBREAK　AFTER　HEARTBREAK　AFTER

HEARTBREAK　AFTER　HEARTBREAK　AFTER　HEARTBREAK　AFTER　HEARTBREAK　AFTER

HEARTBREAK　AFTER　HEARTBREAK　AFTER　HEARTBREAK　AFTER　HEARTBREAK　AFTER

HEARTBREAK　AFTER　HEARTBREAK　AFTER　HEARTBREAK　AFTER　HEARTBREAK

AFTER　HEARTBREAK　AFTER　HEARTBREAK　AFTER　HEARTBREAK　AFTER

HEARTBREAK　AFTER　HEARTBREAK　AFTER　HEARTBREAK

AFTER　HEARTBREAK　AFTER　HEARTBREAK　AFTER

HEARTBREAK　AFTER　HEARTBREAK　AFTER

HEARTBREAK　AFTER　HEARTBREAK

AFTER HEARTBREAK AFTER

HEARTBREAK

AFTER

I FOUND MYSELF

(BLESS) MY BEAUTIFUL (BROKEN) HEART,
WHO TEACHES ME TO SEE
WHAT IS HIDDEN BEFORE ME,
AND LETS ME LISTEN TO THE CHORUS IN MY SOUL;
A NEW KIND OF LOVE SO UNKNOWN TO ME BEFORE

THE SAME (VERY) BEAUTIFUL (BROKEN) HEART
THAT BATHES LOVE IN THE EMBRACE OF COMPASSION
AND BREAKS ME TO THE POINT OF TRANSFORMATION.

FOR ONCE, I THOUGHT I KNEW
WHO I WAS AND HOW TO LOVE,
BUT IT WAS YOU,

MY (VERY) BEAUTIFUL (BROKEN) HEART

WHO PROVED ME OTHERWISE.

I THOUGHT
THERE WOULD NOT BE ANOTHER HEARTBREAK;
MY LIFE IN ITS SOFT, GOLDEN LIGHT,
A NEW DECADE OF BLOOM & GLORY.
YET THERE WAS A DAY,
WHERE THE ONE I LOVE MET WITH SICKNESS
AND DEATH CAME TO VISIT HIM.

BARELY BEING ABLE TO WALK,
ROBBED OF THIS PEACE,
POSSESSED BY DARK FORCES.

OH, MY (VERY) BEAUTIFUL (BROKEN) HEART
LEARNED TO BREAK EVEN THOUGH
MORE GRACEFULLY,

ONE PIECE AT A TIME,
A RAINDROP EVERY SECOND,
YET HIS PAIN DID NOT CEASE,
HIS JOYFUL SPIRIT SO ABSENT.

UNABLE TO SMILE,
I LONGED FOR HIS LAUGHTER.

AND THERE IT WAS,
MY (VERY) BEAUTIFUL (BROKEN) HEART
LETTING ITSELF BREAK
LIKE BREAD INTO A STARVING MOUTH.

WHAT WAS (MY) VERY BEAUTIFUL (BROKEN) HEART TO DO?

CLEAN ITS MARBLE FLOORS BY THE HOUR?
TAKE ITS SPLINTERS OFF ITS OWN HANDS AND FEET?
WIPE ITSELF WITH SILK CARESSES OF SELF—LOVE?

BUT HOW NOT TO BLESS YOU

MY (VERY) BEAUTIFUL (BROKEN) HEART.

IF YOU HAVE GIVEN ME

A ONE-WAY TICKET TO MY SOUL,

WHERE BOTH SORROW AND JOY CAN DANCE FREELY,

WHERE I CAN SIT AND ROMANCE MY OWN TEARS

AND ALSO WALTZ WITH MY TRUEST JOY.

BUT HOW NOT TO LOVE YOU

MY (VERY) BEAUTIFUL (BROKEN) HEART,

IF YOU HAVE TAUGHT ME THAT

HUMANITY LOOKS LIKE ONE

AND I AM FINALLY THE WOMAN

YOU HAVE SOUGHT TO LOVE SO MUCH.

I WOULD NOT BE HERE

WITHOUT YOU,

MY (VERY) BEAUTIFUL (BROKEN) HEART,

SO, I THANK YOU.

AND WHEN MY LOVE COULD NOT WALK,
AND COULD ONLY SHUFFLE HIS FEET,
I LEAPED FOR BOTH OF US,
AND I HELD HIM FROM AFAR WITH MY
SOFT—LIGHTED PRAYERS.

AND WHEN HE COULD NOT TALK,
I SPILLED POETRY ONTO PAGES,
AND I MADE A BOOK OUT OF OUR LOVE.

HOW MANY TIMES CAN A HEART BREAK? — I ASKED GOD.

WHAT SHE MISSED THE MOST ABOUT THEIR LOVE
WAS HIM.

(WHEN SHE FIRST MET HIM.)

WHEN SHE LOST HIM,
SHE DID NOT ONLY
LOSE HER LOVER,
BUT, ALSO HER BEST FRIEND.

SHE LOVED HIM
BECAUSE
HE DID NOT TAKE SO MUCH FROM HER,
BECAUSE
HE GAVE HER SUNLIGHT
AND NEVER ASKED FOR A RAY.

(UNTIL HE TOOK ALL HER SUNSHINE AWAY FROM HER).

SHE WANTED TO FALL IN LOVE WITH HIM AGAIN;
LIKE WHEN THEY MET
LIKE WHEN THEY WERE SO HAPPY.

SHE WANTED TO LOVE HIM AGAIN;
LIKE IN THOSE EARLY YEARS
WHEN NO ONE ELSE EXISTED.
LIKE IN THOSE MOMENTS
HE WAS STILL HEALTHY,
LIKE IN THOSE INSTANCES
THEY WALKED AROUND PARIS
AND LAUGHED
AND MADE LOVE
AND TOLD EACH OTHER JOKES.

SHE WANTED TO BELIEVE IN HIM AGAIN.
(WITH **ALL** OF HER HEART)

SHE KNEW HE WAS AN ADDICT
JUST LIKE HER PARENTS.

SHE KNEW IT,
BUT WHEN SHE MET HIM,
SHE THOUGHT:

"THIS TIME IT WILL BE DIFFERENT."

THE STRONG-WILLED AND WOUNDED GIRL WITHIN HER
TRYING TO CREATE A NEW STORY ABOUT LOVE:

"NOW THAT I AM OLDER AND STRONGER,
I CAN SAVE HIM
LIKE I COULD NOT SAVE MY OWN PARENTS."

UNTIL

SHE UNDERSTOOD THAT
TRYING TO "SAVE" OTHERS
WAS HER WAY TO DELAY
HER OWN HEALING
HER OWN DESTINY
HER HIGHEST POTENTIAL

BECAUSE

SHE WAS ALSO AN ADDICT,
TO AN ADDICT'S LOVE.

HOW MANY TIMES DOES A HEART NEED TO BREAK BEFORE IT
OPENS INTO LIGHT?

WHEN IT IS TOO MUCH BREAKING
   IRREPARABLE,
                UNFIXABLE.

WHEN IS THE HEARTBREAK TOO MUCH TO FIND ONE'S WILL TO
START AGAIN?

FOR IF MY HEART HAS BEEN BROKEN FOR EVERY PENANCE,
I THINK, MY LORD, WE ARE EVEN,
I'VE AMENDED EACH MISTAKE
ALREADY, TWICE.
I MAY SOUND LIKE A VICTIM,
BUT YOU KNOW WE ARE SPEAKING
WITHOUT ANYONE HEARING.

SO, TELL ME:

HOW MUCH RUPTURE IS NEEDED TO FINALLY TRANSFORM?

HOW MANY MORE DO I HAVE LEFT

BEFORE I GO AND SERVE YOU,

BEFORE EACH OF MY HEARTBEATS GO DEEP ONTO THE EARTH

UNTIL I BECOME NOTHINGNESS?

FOR I HAVE FEARED BEING NOTHING ALL OF MY LIFE.

BUT NOW IT IS PROBABLY BETTER

THAN BEING A WALKING BROKEN HEART,

BARELY BREATHING,

AND TRYING TO LOVE.

ONE MORE TIME. 

I SHOULD HAVE WRITTEN A POEM
EVERY DAY
SINCE YOU HAVE BEEN GONE
AND DOCUMENTED EVERY MEMORY
OF YOU,
OF US.

WHEN WAS THE LAST TIME WE LAUGHED?

OUR LAST DATE BEFORE YOU LOST YOUR MIND?

THE LAST TIME WE MADE LOVE MADLY IN LOVE?

I SHOULD HAVE WRITTEN A POEM
EVERY DAY
WHEN WE WERE CONTENT
LIVING OUR DREAM LIFE
BOTH OF US
UNDER THE SPELL
OF HAPPINESS
WE DID NOT KNOW
EPHEMERAL.

WHEN WAS THE LAST TIME WE DANCED?

OUR LAST STUPID FIGHT TO THEN MAKE UP AND LAUGH?

THE LAST TIME WE WENT TO BED PEACEFULLY?

I SHOULD HAVE WRITTEN A POEM
EVERY DAY
SINCE I MET YOU
TO LET THE WORLD KNOW
THAT LOVE IS POSSIBLE,
THAT IT ARRIVES UNEXPECTEDLY,
AND IT CAN WALK IN PARIS
AND MEDITATE IN BALI.
BUT IT CAN ALSO SLEEP ON AIR MATTRESSES
AND EAT PIZZA ON THE FLOOR IN WEST LOS ANGELES.

WHEN WAS THE LAST TIME
I LET YOU KNOW
WITH THE PERFECT WORDS
WITH THE RIGHT CARESSES,

THAT YOU HAVE BEEN

THE MOST BEAUTIFUL

KIND OF LOVE.

I SHOULD HAVE WRITTEN A POEM
ABOUT YOU,
EVERY DAY.

THE DEPTHS OF DESPAIR
YOU HAVE BEEN THERE,
BUT YOU ARE A FIGHTER.

EVEN IN THE MIDST OF AGONY,
YOU KEEP FIGHTING.

(DROPPING MY LOVED ONES AT REHAB —SO MANY TIMES
— WAS HEARTBREAKING).

TO REDUCE MY MOTHER TO
AN ALCOHOLIC IS NOT FAIR
EVEN THOUGH THAT'S WHAT MY PAIN WOULD LIKE ME TO SAY,
BUT SHE IS SO MUCH MORE.

SHE IS AN ARTIST.
A CREATIVE SOUL TRAPPED IN THE WRONG SPAN OF TIME
SURROUNDED BY THE WRONG PEOPLE
A TALENT NOT SEEN SOON ENOUGH
A NEED FOR HER FATHER'S LOVE
GONE TOO SOON TO KNOW
WHAT WAS TRUE LOVE.

TO REDUCE HER TO A DRUG ADDICT IS NOT FAIR:
SPOILED EARLY ON
BY HER HARDWORKING MOTHER;
THE SACRIFICIAL MOTHER
A HIGH—TEMPERED SAINT OF A MOTHER
MY GRANDMOTHER.

A DEEP LOVE TURNED DEPENDENCY
MY MOTHER, THE CENTER OF ATTENTION.

BLUE—EYED AND BLEACHED BLONDE HAIR

GOLDEN AND TONED SKIN
A MODEL.
IN A CULTURE WHERE PHYSICAL BEAUTY
IS IDEALIZED,
TELL HER SHE IS BEAUTIFUL AND
SHE WILL FEEL SHE IS BACK IN THE 80S:
MODEL OF THE YEAR
MAFIA TIMES IN MEDELLÍN.

COCAÍNA & ALCOHOL TOO EARLY ON
COLOMBIA IN THE 80S.

TO REDUCE HER TO BIPOLAR IS NOT FAIR,
MY MOTHER:
SHE IS CHARISMATIC.

IF I LET HER SPEAK RIGHT HERE,
RIGHT NOW,
HE WILL STEAL THE SHOW.
BEFORE I KNOW HOW TO GO ON,
SHE WILL FINISH THE POEM WITH HER HUMOR.

SHE IS THE CONVERSATION STARTER
SHE IS THE FRESH FRUIT IN THE MORNING

(WITH ADDED WHITE SUGAR)
SHE IS THE ORIGINAL DREAMER.

SHE HAS THE 7 LIVES OF A CAT &
SHE IS OBSESSED WITH THE STARS.

SHE STILL DREAMS TO CREATE
LIKE COCO CHANEL
DRAWING DOLLS AND DRESSES
ON ART PAPER AS LONG AS I CAN REMEMBER.

MY MOTHER WAS DIAGNOSED LATER ON IN LIFE
AS BI-POLAR,
YET, NO ONE TOOK IT TOO SERIOUSLY
AT A TIME
WHEN NO ONE TALKED ABOUT MENTAL HEALTH
IN SOUTH AMERICA.

INSTEAD, SHE PRAYED IN BETWEEN RELAPSES
WHEN BLACKOUTS AND NEAR-DEATH EXPERIENCES
NO LONGER ENTICED HER,
AND ABUSIVE MEN LOST
THEIR ENCHANTMENT

TO REDUCE HER TO AN ALCOHOLIC IS NOT FAIR
EVEN THOUGH THAT'S WHAT MY PAIN WOULD LIKE ME TO SAY,
BUT SHE IS SO MUCH MORE;

SHE IS MY MOTHER
THE ONE WHOSE PAIN
GIFTED ME THE GIFT OF LIFE AND POETRY.

(AND SHOULD I ADD: I AM HAPPY TO REPORT SHE HAS BEEN
SOBER FOR TWO YEARS.)

I AM THE END PRODUCT OF ADDICTION:

AN OVERDOSE OF LOVE;

LOVE LIKE WHITE SUGAR.

I AM STILL HERE

HOLDING A SKY OF JOYS

FOR BOTH OF US

UNTIL YOU CAN HOLD

YOUR OWN,

MI AMOR.

WHEN MY LOVE GOT SICK

PERFECTION IN MY EYES,
THE ONE WHO I HAVE GIVEN SOME OF THE BEST
YEARS OF MY LIFE... I COULD NOT ACCEPT IT.

I THOUGHT, IT WILL PASS, LIKE THE OTHER TIMES
WHEN HE STRUGGLED.

WHEN MY LOVE GOT SICK,
PARAMEDICS IN OUR LIVING ROOM
KNEW US BY OUR NAMES &
I OFFERED THEM TEA AT 5 PM &
THEY COMPLIMENTED ME ON HOW
CALM I WAS DESPITE "THE SITUATION,"
AND EVEN MENTIONED THEY TALKED ABOUT ME
AT THE FIRE STATION.

WHEN MY LOVE GOT SICK
HE BECAME A SHELL OF THE MAN I KNEW.
LOST IN HIS PAIN AND SORROW,
INTOXICATED BY HIS GRIEF, LOSING
A NEW PART OF HIMSELF BY THE HOUR.

UNABLE TO WALK WITHOUT TREMORS.

WHERE ONCE THERE WERE MUSCLES,
I SAW BONES.

HE WAS ONLY 40 YEARS OLD.

REGARDLESS, IT FELT GOOD TO KNOW HE WAS STILL ALIVE
THOUGH SOMETIMES, I WONDER, IF TO LIVE
IN SUCH PAIN WAS EVEN WORTH ROLLING THE DICE
ONE MORE TIME.

AFTER ALL, HE WAS YOUNG TO BE IN SUCH CONDITION.
SPIRALING DOWN WITHOUT SLEEP,
AMBULANCE RIDES AND
MEDIOCRE ER CARE DESPITE HIS PRIVILEGE.

A NEW PILL TO SWALLOW.

THE SAME PILLS THAT ARE KILLING MILLIONS MORE
IN AMERICA.

AND WHEN PEOPLE ASKED ABOUT MY LOVE,
THEY WANTED ME TO TELL THEM EXACTLY
WHAT HIS CONDITION WAS,
BUT I COULD NOT TELL THEM.

IT WAS BETTER TO INVENT SOMETHING MORE PALATABLE,
A STORY WITHIN A STORY,
BECAUSE UNLESS SOMEONE LIVES IT, HOW CAN THEY GET IT?

BESIDES, IT'S NOT THEIR BUSINESS.
BESIDES, IT IS HIS STORY.
BESIDES, IT IS SO EASY TO JUDGE.

BECAUSE TO LOVE OUR LOVED ONES' SHADOWS
IS TO LEARN TO LOVE OUR OWN.
AND WHO WANTS TO DO THAT...
UNLESS ONE HAS TO.

WHEN MY LOVE GOT SICKER,
I UNDERSTOOD THE MEANING OF TOTAL SURRENDER.
WHEN I SAW THERE WAS NOTHING IN THE WHOLE WORLD
I COULD DO TO ALLEVIATE HIS PAIN,
WHEN THERE WAS NO WAY
TO "SAVE HIM"
TO "FIX" THE SITUATION
BUT TO RIDE THE WAVE OF DESTINY
AND PRAY, WHITE CANDLE ON MY MANY ALTARS.

AND

WHEN MY LOVE GOT THE SICKEST,
I LEARNED TO BE ALONE
AND TAKE MYSELF ON DATES PEOPLE SAW AS INSTAGRAM
VACATIONS.

SERENADED MYSELF AND MADE LOVE TO LIFE IN EVERY WAY.

I LEARNED TO LOVE MY MIND.

I LEARNED TO LOVE ME SO MUCH MORE.

TO CARE FOR MY SOUL AND FOR MY BODY.

SECURE MY PEACE AS MY SOUL'S FORTRESS
AS I WAITED.

3 YEARS HOLDING ON TO OUR LOVELY MEMORIES
AS POLAROIDS OF ETERNAL HAPPINESS.

TODAY,

IT IS ACCURATE TO SAY:

WE ARE JUST A BEAUTIFUL MEMORY.

I MADE THE DECISION TO WAKE UP A BIT EARLIER.
WIN MY GENTLE BATTLE WITH MY OH—SO—FUNCTIONAL
DEPRESSION.

8 AM

I WARM UP MY TEA, MEDITATE
& LIT UP MY SAGE AND PRAY.
LOKAH SAMASTAH SUKHINO BHAVANTU
MAY ALL BEINGS INCLUDING MYSELF BE
HAPPY, PEACEFUL AND FREE OF SUFFERING

10 AM

YOU ARE STILL SLEEPING.

MY FIRST REACTION IS TO BE ANNOYED.

WHY IN THE WORLD ARE YOU STILL SLEEPING?

WHY ARE THE CURTAINS STILL CLOSED,

AND WHEN WILL YOU LET A BIT OF SUNSHINE ENTER OUR

BEDROOM?

NOW, I UNDERSTAND WHEN YOU TELL ME THAT WHEN A WAVE
OF DEPRESSION COMES,
IT'S AS IF A GIANT ELEPHANT IS SITTING ON TOP OF YOUR
CHEST.

10:30 AM

I HAVE FINISHED SIPPING ON MY TEA.
MAYBE I CAN NOW TAKE OUR DOG OUT FOR A WALK,
GET OUT OF YOUR WAY
SO YOU CAN HAVE YOUR MOMENT.

I AM KEEPING MYSELF IN A GOOD MOOD.

11 AM

I TAKE THE LONGER ROUTE
SO I CAN GIVE YOU SOME TIME
TO WAKE UP IN SILENCE,

PERHAPS SHOWER,

AND PUT YOUR THOUGHTS AWAY FOR A SHORT VACATION OR
EVEN A SABBATICAL.

AS FOR ME,
I AM STILL ON A POSITIVE NOTE.

FOR HALF AN HOUR MORE...

IT'S 12 NOON.

NOW,
THE DARKNESS OF OUR BEDROOM
OBSCURES MY OWN HOPE AND IT'S NOT EVEN TIME FOR LUNCH.

I CLOSE THE DOOR.

1 PM

I TAKE MYSELF FOR LUNCH.
GO OUTDOORS,
TRY TO GET SOME WORK DONE.

BUT HAVE YOU EATEN?
I ORDERED LUNCH FOR YOU AND I DELIVER IT.

2 PM

YOU ARE UP NOW
BUT FEELING GUILTY.
YOU FEEL LIKE YOU SHOULD BE DOING A MILLION AND ONE
THINGS
TO FEEL BETTER,
TO BE BETTER.

YOU LOOK AT YOUR DESK AND
YOU FIND A LONG LIST OF SELF—CARE ITEMS.
ALL UNATTENDED.

I'M HANGING IN THERE.

3 PM

I TEXT YOU AS I GO ON MY WELLNESS
MENTAL HEALTH WALK.
ARE YOU OK?
HOW ARE YOU FEELING?

I AM FEELING DEPLETED.

4 PM

I AM TEMPTED TO ASK YOU AGAIN.
I AM TEMPTED TO PREACH TO YOU AGAIN.
I AM TEMPTED TO TELL YOU WHAT TO DO AGAIN.

BUT NOW, I KNOW A LITTLE BETTER. THIS IS CO-DEPENDENCY.

I RE-CENTER MYSELF.
OM MANE PADME HUM
LOKAH SAMASTAH SUKHINO BHAVANTU
MAY ALL BEINGS, INCLUDING MYSELF,
BE HAPPY, PEACEFUL, AND FREE OF SUFFERING.

DEPRESSION   IS   NOT   LAZINESS.
DEPRESSION IS A DISEASE SHELTERED IN THE HOUSE OF
TRAUMA.
DEPRESSION IS THE MISTRESS ENTERING UNINVITED,
WALKING AROUND OUR HOUSE LIKE A QUEEN,
WITH NO KINGDOM.

TOUCHING HERSELF ON EVERY SOFA.
HAVING ORGASMS ON OUR WEDDING BED.

SHE HAS TAKEN OVER.
SHE EVEN TAKES A BUBBLE BATH AND INSISTS ON HAVING
CHAMPAGNE.

SHE IS THAT KIND OF A BITCH.

RUTHLESS.
SHE EVEN TRIED TO WALK IN HIGH HEELS
OVER OUR MEMORIES,
ON ALL THE GOOD TIMES WE'VE HAD
BEFORE SHE CAME INTO OUR LIVES.

BUT SHE DOES NOT KNOW ME.
I AM AS RUTHLESS AS SHE IS.
THAT LOVE GENE THAT WILL DROWN DARKNESS WITH A KISS.

DEPRESSION FLEES ME.
SHE PANICS AROUND ME
BUT NOT AROUND HIM.

AROUND HIM, SHE CONTROLS HIM
LIKE A WEAPON OF MASS DESTRUCTION.

DEPRESSION, THAT BITCH IS SO CLINGY.

SHE DECIDED TO STAY WAY TOO LONG.
AND I'M NOT FEEDING HER.

THE OVEREXTENDED GUEST
NO ONE INVITED

9PM

I TURN OFF YOUR LIGHT
MAKE SURE YOU ARE ALL RIGHT
& STILL BREATHING
YOU ARE SO HIGHLY MEDICATED.

I CRY ALONE WHEN NO ONE CAN SEE ME.

10 PM

I STAY UP FOR ABOUT TWO MORE HOURS.

I WRITE OR TRY TO...

HOW IT WAS
HOW IT FELT
BEFORE DEPRESSION CAME TO TAKE YOU AWAY FROM ME.

A LOVE SO STRONG IT DID NOT FEEL REAL.
A LOVE SO GOOD IT FELT LIKE AN OUT-OF-BODY EXPERIENCE.

BUT HERE WE ARE AND WE ARE NOT THE ONLY ONES:

(THIS IS WHAT A SMALL AND VAGUE DESCRIPTION OF HOW A
"NORMAL DAY" CAN GO WHEN SOMEONE STRUGGLES WITH CLIN-
ICAL DEPRESSION & A LOVED ONE BECOMES THEIR CAREGIVER.
280 MILLION PEOPLE AROUND THE WORLD SUFFER FROM CLINICAL
DEPRESSION.)

NOTHING IN LIFE PREPARES YOU FOR
THE MOMENT WHEN A LOVED ONE IN
YOUR LIFE BECOMES MENTALLY ILL.

NO ONE PREPARES YOU IN LIFE FOR THAT MOMENT WHEN A LOVED ONE STRUGGLES WITH ADDICTION.

TO THE BOYS WHOSE HEARTS I BROKE ...
I AM SORRY.

LET ME TELL YOU I'VE PAID EVERY OUNCE OF YOUR PAIN.

I DID NOT HAVE THE COURAGE TO WALK AWAY
WHEN IT WAS TIME TO SAY:

THIS IS ENOUGH,
MY SOUL IS ALREADY GONE.

LET ME WALK AWAY
I NEED A NEW DIRECTION.
MY SPIRIT CRAVES NEW ANSWERS
& WE HAVE NEW INTENTIONS.

TO THE BOYS WHOSE HEARTS I BROKE ...
I AM SORRY.
I DID NOT KNOW ANY BETTER
AND SOMETIMES, I DID.
I FELT LIKE I CARED FOR YOU,
AND I COULD NOT LET GO,
I WAS SELFISH.

BELIEVE ME WHEN I TELL YOU THAT
I'VE PAID EVERY OUNCE OF YOUR PAIN.

I MISSED YOU TERRIBLY.
WHEN THERE WAS NOTHING I COULD DO
AND I WROTE TO YOU AND FOR YOU,
EVEN IF YOU NEVER READ IT.

I EVEN DREAMED ABOUT YOU.
IN THOSE DREAMS,
WE WERE BACK TOGETHER
AND ALL OUR PAIN WAS GONE
AND YOU AND I GOT
A SECOND CHANCE,
A NEW LIFE,
SOMEWHERE IN MADRID
BEFORE DESPAIR
TOOK US UNDER HIS WINGS.

BECAUSE
I CAN TELL
THE BOYS WHOSE HEARTS I BROKE ...

I DID TRULY LOVE YOU

TO THE BOYS WHO BROKE MY HEART,
YOU MAY STILL THINK ABOUT ME SOMETIMES
& LOOK ME UP ONLINE
&
THINK,
WHAT COULD HAVE BEEN OF OUR LIVES IF WE'D STAYED
TOGETHER?

YOU LEFT WAY BEFORE I FOUND MY FORTUNE,
AND BY THAT, I MEAN
BEFORE I FOUND MY PURPOSE.

IMAGINE HOW MUCH BETTER I LOVE NOW
THAT I KNOW WHO I AM,
THAT I KNOW WHAT I'M WORTH,
THAT I DON'T NEED YOU.

WHAT DO YOU FEEL WHEN YOU CLICK AND CLICK
AND SEE ME ACCOMPLISHING THESE THINGS,
I'VE ALWAYS DREAMED?

SEEING THOSE DREAMS — I USED TO TALK TO YOU ABOUT — ALL
MANIFESTED?

AIN'T I SO POWERFUL?
WASN'T MY LOVE ENOUGH FOR YOU?

I KNOW I WAS WEAK WHEN YOU KISSED ME,
YOU HAD THIS WAY OF KNOWING
TO MAKE ME
FALL IN LOVE WITH YOU SO MADLY.

LOVE YOU MADLY, I DID.

NOW I KNOW:

YOU COULD HAVE NEVER SATISFIED MY SOUL,
YOU SEE, YOU ARE STILL THE SAME,
I, ON THE OTHER HAND,
HAVE FLOWN MILLIONS OF MILES AWAY.

I'VE BLESSED MY OWN TEARS WITH BOTH JOY AND SORROW,
BUT YOU CHOSE TO TAKE THE EASIEST WAY.

WHAT YOU THOUGHT WOULD GIVE YOU SATISFACTION.

I, MY ONCE—LOVE,

DON'T CRAVE DOMESTICITY,

I, MY ONCE—LOVE,
DON'T CRAVE DOMESTICITY,

I AM MADE UP OF PURE PASSION.

YOU HIDE FROM YOURSELF,
I SEEK MY OWN EXPANSION.

YOU FORGOT WHO YOU ARE.
LET ME REMIND YOU,
THAT I THOUGHT YOU WERE
THE BEST. I SAW IN YOU SUCH GRACE.

FOR ME, ALL YOUR DREAMS MEANT
YOU WOULD GO FOR THEM,
YOU COULD HAVE BEEN
WHAT YOU ALWAYS DREAMED.

YOU SEE,
I SAW THE BEST OF YOU IN ME,
I SAW MORE IN YOU THAN YOU SAW IN ME.

BUT

TO THE BOYS WHO BROKE MY HEART,
I AM SO GRATEFUL.
I WOULD NOT BE THIS VERSION OF ME
IF IT WAS NOT BECAUSE OF ALL THOSE TEARS.

I WOULD NOT BE HERE,
LIVING MY DREAMS
BECAUSE WITH MY WINGS CLIPPED,
I WOULD NOT LIVE SO FREE,
BEING FINALLY ME.

WHO IS GOING TO HOLD YOUR PAIN WHEN THINGS GET ROUGH
ALONG THE WAY?

   — HE ASKED ME.

NO ONE IS HERE TO BEAR OUR PAIN,
BUT THERE IS SOMETHING I KNOW:

IN TIMES OF DEEP SORROW,
THE COMPANY OF OTHER WOMEN & FEMMES IS
ESSENTIAL. — I ANSWERED.

I FIXED ALL THE BROKEN
PLACES INSIDE OUR HOME.
PAINTED OVER CRACKED CORNERS,
TOOK DOWN OLD LIGHT FIXTURES,
COLORED OUR WALLS,
LIT MY INDIAN INCENSE
COPAL & PALO SANTO,
WATERED OUR PLANTS,
TALKED TO THEM
& PLAYED THEM MUSIC.

I PAINTED OUR KITCHEN
WHITE
& BROUGHT EXOTIC
FLOWERS INSIDE...

I'VE FIXED ALL THE BROKEN PLACES
INSIDE OUR HOME,
TRYING TO
FIX OUR BROKENNESS.

WISHING I COULD
PAINT YOUR PAIN,
BRIGHT YELLOW

& SOW A GARDEN
IN YOUR HEART
WHERE SUNFLOWERS
DANCE
& SMILE.

I WISH I COULD FIX
YOUR BROKENNESS,
BUT HOW CAN I
IF I AM ALSO
WORKING ON
MENDING MINE.

I KNEW WE WERE NOT GOING ANYWHERE.
THERE WAS NO DESTINATION
WHERE WE COULD SAFELY ARRIVE,
AND WE BOTH KNEW THAT
FROM THE VERY START.

BUT I WAS OPEN TO THE JOURNEY
TO THE DAY—TO—DAY MOMENTS
THAT LIFE WOULD GIFT US
THE BREAD OF LOVE
IN THE MIDDLE OF THE DAY.

I KNEW WE WERE NOT GOING ANYWHERE.
THERE WAS NO CITY, NO STREET
WHERE WE WOULD EVER LIVE
OR EVEN STAY FOR TOO LONG.

BUT I INNOCENTLY THOUGHT
THAT WHAT WE WERE LIVING
WAS SO STRONG THAT
IT DID NOT MATTER,
THAT IT WAS WORTH
THE BUTTERFLIES,
EVERYTHING.

EVEN YOUR TEXTS

OR

WHEN

I SAW YOU

OR

WHEN I KISSED YOU

OR

WHEN I TOUCHED YOUR SKIN

AND TOOK MYSELF

ON DREAMY MEDITATIONS

OF SUCH SWEET PLEASURE.

I KNEW WE WERE NOT GOING ANYWHERE,

BUT SOMEHOW, I DREAMED

THIS DREAM OF LOVE WITH YOU ALONE

ALL ON MY OWN.

MY HEART IS A FRIEND OF FIRE; PAIN CAN REACH SUCH PEAKS
THAT AFTER A WHILE YOU CAN'T
REALLY FEEL.
YOU KEEP MOVING
HOPING THE FLAMES WILL
EXTINGUISH AS YOU WALK.

SOLVE WHAT'S NECESSARY,
A SURVIVOR'S MENTALITY:
YOU DRINK THE ASHES
OF YOUR OWN
HEART

AND WHEN YOU LOOK UP,
A TREE COOLS YOU DOWN
AND CENTERS YOU IN
INNER TRUTH.

WHEN PAIN IS UNBEARABLE,
WHEN HOPE IS LOST,
REMIND YOURSELF:

AS FIRE, COMO EL FUEGO

WARMS, CALIENTA,

MI ALMA, MY SOUL,

SO IT CAN DESTROY

ALL IT FINDS AROUND,

GIVE IT BACK TO THE SOIL,

CALL IT ETHER,

LIFE'S CYCLES

RECLAIM YOURSELF

AS MANY TIMES AS NECESSARY.

I KEPT LOOKING FOR YOU
WISHING YOU WOULD WALK BY THAT DOOR
AND YOUR SMILE WOULD LIGHT MY WORLD ON FIRE.

I KEPT WONDERING IF YOUR ABSENCE WAS FEAR
OR A CONSCIOUS CHOICE, NO EXCUSES
IN THE NAME OF LOVE.

AND THOUGH YOUR SILENCE WAS SO CLEAR
I WISHED YOU WOULD WRITE TO ME
& INVITE ME FOR A DRINK UNDER THE FULL MOON
AND MAKE LOVE INSIDE THE WOODS.

BUT YOU NEVER CAME,
& YOU NEVER MET ME HALFWAY,
AND HERE I AM STILL WONDERING
WHERE AND WHY YOU CAME INTO MY LIFE
IF WE WERE GOING NOWHERE.

IT WAS NOT THAT I WAS NOT ENOUGH OR I WAS MISSING SOMETHING; IT WAS YOU WHO WAS NOT READY TO BE LOVED BY A LOVE LIKE MINE. OR WAS IT THE UNIVERSE SAVING ME FROM SOMETHING SO PAINFUL BY MAKING ME UNDESIRABLE IN YOUR EYES SO YOU COULD NOT HURT ME? I WILL NEVER KNOW, BUT WHAT I DO KNOW IS THAT WHEN I LOVED YOU, HOW MUCH I WISHED TO BE WHOMEVER YOU WANTED ME TO BE AND MORPH INTO AS MANY FORMS AS YOU DESIRED, SO I COULD BE THE ONE THAT WENT TO BED WITH YOU EACH NIGHT AND SAW YOU WHEN I FIRST OPENED MY EYES. AND THOUGH I STARTED TO DOUBT MYSELF, THINKING OF MY FLAWS AS MY MISTAKES, EVEN QUESTIONING MY AGE TO PLEASE YOUR TASTE, I AM SLOWLY STARTING TO REALIZE THAT I AM THE KIND OF LOVE, ONLY A FEW WILL EVER GET A CHANCE TO EXPERIENCE.

I AM THAT WOMAN THAT CHOOSES TO LIVE IN THE PRESENT, ONE BREATH AT A TIME, EMBRACING IT ALL SO AS NOT TO MISS AN INSTANT, SO TO ASK THE UNIVERSE TO REWIND AND TO TAKE ME BACK TO THAT TIME WHEN YOU AND I...?

IS THAT TOO MUCH?

BECAUSE SINCE YOU LEFT, I KEEP STRUGGLING TO COME BACK TO THIS VERY INSTANT WHERE YOU ARE NOWHERE TO BE FOUND

AND

(I TRULY MISS YOU.)

THE ACHE

THAT UNEXPLAINABLE HOLE IN YOUR CHEST
THAT EMPTINESS IN YOUR BELLY
THAT FIRE THAT COMES IN WAVES
THAT LONGING THAT DROPS YOU TO YOUR KNEES
THAT PRAYER THAT BECOMES A SUPPLICATION FOR
THE ONE YOU LOVE TO RETURN.

THE NEGOTIATIONS WITH GOD IF HE WAS TO BRING YOU BACK
THE DESTRUCTION OF YOUR PRIDE FOR THAT "ONE MORE TIME"
THE ENEMY OF REASON
THIS CONSTANT MISSING YOU
HAS BECOME THE CONSTANT ACHE
I TRY TO SOOTHE WITH LIFE'S GRACE.

YOU BROUGHT ME SO MUCH HAPPINESS
BUT ALSO MUCH PAIN...

HOW DO I RECONCILE THAT?

WE WERE NEVER ANYTHING.
NO NAME, NO HOUSE
WITH OUR NAMES.

WE WERE JUST A FEW DAYS OF FUN TURNED BITTER
A FEW SUNSETS EATEN BY A BLACK HOLE
AND A FEW HUNDRED KISSES DROWN AT THE BOTTOM OF MY
SOUL.

WHAT DO I MISS ABOUT US?

WHAT NEVER HAPPENED, WHAT WE DID NOT GET TO LIVE —THE
CUT—TOO—SHORT MAGICAL MOMENTS— WE COULD HAVE HAD IF
YOU HAD LET THEM IN, BUT YOU GOT AFRAID TOO QUICKLY.

AFRAID OF THE RADIANCE OF MY LOVE, THE LIGHT COMING
THROUGH YOUR WINDOW, LOOKING AT THE POSSIBILITY THAT
YOU TOO COULD FEEL THIS LOVE JUST AS BEAUTIFUL.

HEARTBREAK CAN HARDEN YOU
BUT IT CAN ALSO MAKE YOU SOFTER.

IT CAN MAKE YOU CYNICAL
OR IT CAN BATHE YOU WITH HUMILITY.

AND IT CAN LOCK YOUR HEART SO TIGHT
THAT THE LIGHT NEVER REACHES IT.

BUT IS SUCH PAIN WORTH IT,
OF KILLING YOUR GOD–GIVEN
ABILITY TO LOVE DEEPLY?

HEARTBREAK MAY END UP MAKING YOU

AN ADVENTURER

A SEEKER

A PHILANTHROPIST

A BETTER VERSION OF YOURSELF

AND

A MORE COMPASSIONATE HUMAN.

ONE DAY
I WON'T BE AFRAID TO BE LOVED AGAIN
AND I WILL LET YOUR HANDS CARESS MINE WITHOUT PULLING
BACK

I WILL BEGIN TO TRUST YOU AGAIN
WHEN YOU STOP BY TO OFFER ME CAFÈ IN THE MORNING
OR SURPRISINGLY PASS ME BY TO KISS ME AND
SAY HELLO.

ONE DAY,
I WILL BE ABLE TO RECEIVE IT ALL.
NOT PULL AWAY FROM LOVE'S KINDNESS,
BELIEVE WHEN IT WANTS TO
SERVE ME
BREAKFAST
& MAKE THE BED
& RUN ERRANDS
& GO TO BED AT THE SAME TIME
& BRING ME WATER
& PATIENTLY WAIT FOR ME
& WHISPER: I AM BACK
I NEVER REALLY LEFT...
YET.

IT IS HARD TO BELIEVE AGAIN
WHEN ADDICTION HAS
ROBBED ME

SO MANY TIMES

OF THE ONES I LOVE.

MY BODY
WHAT IF I HAD THAT BODY
AND THAT BODY WOULD MAKE HIM STAY?

HOW BRUTALLY IRONIC TO FALL IN LOVE WITH A BODY,
WITH THE PART OF US THAT ROTS AS SOON AS THE SKIN GETS
COLD?

BUT
WHAT IS IT ABOUT OUR BODIES,
THAT MAKES IT SEEM LIKE THEY ARE THE ONLY
REALITY OF US?

FOR WHEN WAS SOMEONE JUST IN LOVE WITH YOUR SOUL,

OR YOU FELT SO MADLY IN LOVE WITH SOMEONE'S SPIRIT?

HOW TO LOVE THE UNSEEN,
INTANGIBLE
PART OF YOU AND OTHERS. 

HOW CAN YOU LOVE THE
UNTOUCHABLE
UNREACHABLE PARTS OF ME
THAT I LONG TO GIVE YOU?

BUT THIS BODY IS BOTH A TEMPLE AND A PRISON.
THIS BODY, THOUGH PERFECT, THEY HAVE TAUGHT IT
HAS FLAWS AND IT LACKS WHAT'S TO BE DESIRED.

MY BODY, THE ONE I GAVE YOU AS AN OFFERING

BECAUSE HOW ELSE CAN I MELT INTO YOUR BEING
IF IT IS NOT THROUGH A KISS AND THESE CARESSES NOW SO
ABSENT?

YOUR SMILE WAS MY WAY TO HOLD ON TO THE ETERNAL PART OF
YOU SO EARTHLY, YOU THE ONE WHO IS SO FAR FROM LOVING
PEOPLE'S SOULS AND MORE USED TO LOVING THEIR BODIES,
BUT HOW ELSE CAN WE REALLY TOUCH EACH OTHER, IF NOT IN
PURE PRESENCE?

MY BODY
WHAT IF I HAD THAT BODY?
WOULD YOU LOVE ME MORE
IF I HAD THAT BODY?

THE PROBLEM IS, I AM SO MUCH MORE.

ONE DAY
IT IS ALL IT TOOK
FOR YOU
TO ERASE
THIS NOTHINGNESS
THAT FELT LIKE
EVERYTHING
BETWEEN US.

THERE IS THIS PLACE I WANTED TO TAKE YOU TO WATCH THE
SUNSET UP IN THE MOUNTAINS BEFORE WE SAID GOODBYE.

IN FACT, THERE WERE MANY PLACES, I DREAMED OF TAKING
YOU TO SHOW YOU MY SIDE OF THE WORLD IN A CITY FILLED
WITH CONTRASTS.

I WANTED MORE SUNRISES WAKING UP NEXT TO YOU AND MORE
SUNSETS AS WE CHEERED FOR A NEW MAGICAL DAY GONE BY.

A DAY FILLED WITH ROMANCE AND LAUGHTER AS WE DROVE BY,
BLASTING OUR FAVORITE MUSIC WITH OUR WINDOWS DOWN.

THERE ARE SO MANY MOMENTS, I AM STILL REPLAYING IN MY
MIND WISHING THEY COULD HAVE COME THROUGH FOR YOU
AND ME, BUT I STILL TRY NOT TO BE ROBBED OF THIS BEAUTIFUL
PRESENT.

A PRESENT THAT DOES NOT SEE YOU NEARBY
AND PERHAPS EVEN A LITTLE FURTHER AWAY EACH DAY THAT
PASSES BY...

BUT I HAVE LIVED LONG ENOUGH TO KNOW THAT IF YOU
WANTED TO BE HERE, YOU WOULD,
SO THERE GOES MY ANSWER.

AND THOUGH YOU COULD ARGUE, YOU STILL ARE COLORING MY
PRESENT AS I MISS YOU.
WE ARE STILL JUST AN INEXISTENT STORY WRITTEN BY ME.

BUT...

AT LEAST, I GOT A LITTLE POEM OUT OF IT.

GOLDEN SAND IN MY HANDS,
MOLECULES AS TINY AS YOUR THOUGHTS OF ME,
SWEET SUMMER BREEZE.

MY LOVE OF YOU,
SUNLIGHT ON MY LIPS.

WILL I ALWAYS FEEL SO BROKEN
WHILE KNOWING I AM WHOLE?

I BROUGHT US ALIVE
FROM ANOTHER LIFETIME.
BUT, HERE ON EARTH,
YOU ARE NOWHERE TO BE FOUND.

SOULMATE LOST IN MY PRAYERS.

GOD

WHISPERING:

"I AM PREPARING YOU FOR A LIFETIME
OF DREAMS DREAMED LIGHT YEARS
BEFORE YOU."

ONE DAY
YOU WAKE UP
AND YOU ARE REMINDED
THAT THERE IS STILL A LOT
OF INNER HEALING TO DO.

THERE ARE A FEW OPTIONS:
1. TO HUMBLY SURRENDER
2. TO ACCEPT THE INEVITABLE INNER WORK AHEAD.
3. TO IGNORE THE CALL

WHICH ONE WILL YOU CHOOSE?

THE ONES WHO BREAK OUR HEARTS
KILL US

TEMPORARILY

YET
SIMULTANEOUSLY,
BRING US BACK TO OURSELVES

AND

IT IS THANKS TO THIS PAIN
THAT WE CAN BE REBORN AGAIN.

LET'S BEGIN AGAIN,
AFTER THE CATASTROPHE OF TRUTH
OF WHO WE ARE.
NOT JUST YOU, BUT I.

I, AS I AM TODAY,
YOU, AS YOU ARE NOW.

LET'S BEGIN AGAIN,

KNOWING

OUR LOVE HAS STAYED TO HELP US
FIND OUR HIGHEST SELVES.

LET'S TRY AGAIN

TO GET LOST
ON THE SAME LAWN,

WHERE WAVES AND BIRDS
SANG TO US
WHEN THEY BARELY
KNEW US.

LET'S START AGAIN.,

A ONE—NIGHT STAND,

LITTLE BLACK DRESS ON THE FLOOR,

& HIGH HEELS IN THE AIR...

A LOVE LIKE OURS,

SEASONS OF GOLDEN SUNSETS

& UNEXPECTED STORMS.

YET, WE ARE STILL HERE

&

THAT'S THE STRENGTH OF OUR LOVE.

GURUS WILL TELL US WE ARE COMPLETE.
WE ARE LOVE; THEREFORE WE CAN'T LACK LOVE.
AND IT ALL SOUNDS LIKE MAGIC TO ME,
AND IT MAKES SENSE,
BUT THEN WHY DO I FEEL SO INCOMPLETE
WITHOUT YOU? SIN TÍ?
THESE DAYS, IT FEELS LIKE I AM A BEGGAR
WAITING FOR YOU TO GIVE ME A SIGN OF YOUR LOVE
WISHING FOR A SHORT MESSAGE OR A CALL
BUT IF I HAVE IT ALL,

WHY DO I CONTINUE TO FEEL THIS WAY WITHOUT YOU?

MY TWO FRENEMIES
FEAR AND ANXIETY

IT'S BEEN DECADES SINCE I FIRST MET THEM.

I WAS 7 OR 8.
MY GRANDMOTHER TELLS ME I AM GOING TO BE OK.

TO BREATHE ONE MORE TIME & I WOULD BE JUST FINE.

NO ONE EVER SPOKE OF
PANIC ATTACKS IN THE 80'S IN COLOMBIA,

ESPECIALLY NOT IN OUR HOUSEHOLD,
WHERE MY GRANDMA WAS A WARRIOR.

TAKE PAIN AS IT COMES AND
KEEP MOVING.

THE WHEELS CAN'T STOP TURNING.

JUST BREATHE ONE MORE TIME
—SHE WOULD SAY STANDING NEXT TO ME INSIDE OUR GUEST
BATHROOM.

—I CAN'T BREATHE— I WOULD TELL HER.
SILENTLY, I WOULD TELL GOD NOT TO TAKE ME.

THAT'S WHEN I MET BOTH FEAR & ANXIETY ON THE SAME DAY.

YOU COULD TELL ME THAT'S ENOUGH TO MAKE ANYONE INSANE.

BUT HERE IS THE THING
YOU SOON REALIZE

THERE IS SOMETHING INSIDE YOURSELF
FILLED WITH STRENGTH AND GOD'S GRACE.
OTHERWISE, HOW COULD YOU TELL
YOURSELF THAT IS NOT THE END JUST YET
WHEN YOU ARE 7 OR 8?

THE BEAUTY OF HEARTBREAK IS THAT IT HUMBLES US.

IT BRINGS OUR EGO TO ITS KNEES.

IT REMINDS US TO PRAY, TO INVOKE A DIVINE FORCE GREATER THAN OURSELVES.

IT BRINGS US FACE TO FACE WITH THE EPHEMERAL NATURE OF OUR OWN LIVES.

AND EVEN THOUGH IT MAKES US AWARE OF THE TREMENDOUS RESILIENCE OF OUR HEARTS

AND HOW POWERFUL WE ARE, IT CONFIRMS THAT WE ARE NOT GOD.

NOW, IT'S YOUR TURN. LET'S HEAL TOGETHER.
I HAVE WRITTEN DOWN SOME PROMPTS TO HELP YOU NAVIGATE
YOUR OWN HEARTBREAK (PROMISE, IT SHALL PASS).

A LIST OF HEARTBREAKS

(FEEL FREE TO WRITE DOWN YOURS AND MAKE ART OUT OF
THEM.)

LOSING YOU MADE ME.....

____

____

____

____

____

____

____

____

____

____

____

____

____

____

____

LOSING YOU MADE ME.....

BREAKING MY OWN HEART HAS SHOWN ME...

BREAKING MY OWN HEART HAS SHOWN ME...

WHAT HAS HEARTBREAK TAUGHT ME ABOUT MYSELF SO FAR?

WHAT MESSAGES DOES MY HEART HAVE FOR ME TODAY?

HEARTBREAK IS TRANSFORMING ME AND AWAKENING ME IN
UNEXPECTED WAYS...

____

____

____

____

____

____

____

____

____

____

____

____

____

____

HEARTBREAK IS TRANSFORMING ME AND AWAKENING ME IN
UNEXPECTED WAYS...

HOW CAN I BE GENTLE AND LOVING WITH MYSELF DURING THIS SEASON?

PART 2

AND THEN... ONE DAY

SHE BEGINS TO HEAL...

MAY MY HEART ALWAYS RECOGNIZE

THE LOVING FROM THE UNKIND

I WONDER,
WHAT'S THE NAME OF THAT PLACE
WHERE MY SOUL
CAN COMPREHEND ITS WINGS
ARE ALREADY GOLDEN?

THERE IS NO MORE TIME
THAN TODAY.

WHY WONDER
IF IT'S HERE OR THERE?

THIS LOVE WHO'S SO CLOSE
OR THE ONE WHO IS FAR AWAY?

IT IS ALL THE SAME
AS LONG AS PEACE GIFTS ME
THIS AWARENESS TO BE
HERE FULLY PRESENT.

THE SUN SETS
AND SO DO ALL MY WORRIES.

WHY HOLD ON TO THE IMPOSSIBLE
WHEN THERE IS NOTHING TO CONTROL
AND WHEN YOU EMBRACE THE FLOW
YOU FINALLY BEGIN TO GROW?

WE ARE JUST LIKE FLOWERS
MOLECULES OF LIGHT
FLOATING SO ALIVE

THE GIFT OF PURE LOVE AND CONNECTION

EQUANIMITY MAY BE THE GOAL
BUT HOW ABOUT JOY AND HEALTHY PLEASURE?

JUST REMEMBER TO LET IT GO
IF IT'S TIME
TO DEPART.

NOTHING IS REALLY OURS;

IT IS JUST BORROWED.
LIGHT IN FRONT OF OUR EYES.
SO LET'S ENJOY IT
UNTIL SUNRISE.

I HOPE YOU CAN SEE IN ME
EVERYTHING
YOU ARE.
WE ARE ALL THE SAME.
DON'T YOU SEE IT?

AS IF YOU DID NOT EXIST,
THAT'S HOW I FINALLY FEEL.

BREATHING IN AS IF IT WAS SPRING.
NOT THAT OVERHEATED SUMMER OF GRIEF
WHAT A RELIEF!

AM I NOSTALGIC?
DO I MISS YOU?

AT TIMES,
YOU STILL COME FLASHING BY
MY MIND.

I CAN SEE YOU FROM AFAR
LIVING YOUR LIFE IN THE SAME CITY
WITHOUT WANTING TO KNOW WHERE YOU LIVE,
OR IMAGINE WHERE YOU WOULD BE

SO, YOU COULD SAY I AM FINALLY FREE.

F
   R
      E
        E

OF THAT SORROW,

THAT CAME WITH YOU
AS EXTRA LUGGAGE.
F
   R
      E
        E

OF ALL THOSE TEARS
I HAVE BURIED DOWN
SO, NO ONE COULD SEE THEM.
F
   R
      E
        E

FROM A LOVE SO POISONOUS
FOR MY SOUL,
A METAPHYSICAL EQUATION
NEVER SOLVED IN MY CORAZÓN.

BECAUSE I HAD TO
TAKE FULL ACCOUNTABILITY
OF THE MESS
I CREATED FOR MYSELF.

THE PROBLEM IS;
I JUMPED INTO ALL OF THIS
TOO QUICKLY,

TRYING TO FILL A VOID
THAT COULD ONLY
BE FILLED WITH LOTS OF
SELF—LOVE.

SO
AT THE END,
LET ME JUST CHEER FOR MYSELF.
THIS PRESENT SENSE
OF INNER PEACE
THAT DETACHMENT FROM YOU
IS BRINGING ME

F
  R
    E
      E
        D
          O
            M

BREAKING IS EASY,
UN—BREAKING IS HARD.

UN—BREAK MI CORAZÓN.
SOOTHE IT WITH ÍCAROS BY THE SUNLIGHT
AS WAVES COME CRASHING BY.

UN—BREAK MI CORAZÓN.
BRING IT STARLIGHT UNDER A DESERT SKY
AND OFFER IT WARM TEA WITH CINNAMON
AS A POTION OF LIGHT.

BREAKING MYSELF IS SO EASY,
BUT THE UN—BREAKING IS PAINFULLY HARD.

SURPRISE ME WITH THE EMBRACE OF ABUELA'S ARMS,
& DRUMS PLAYED PASSIONATELY & JOYFULLY.

LET ME KISS THE MOUNTAINS THAT SUSTAIN ME
PAIN PAINTING ROSES WITH MY TEARS.

BREAKING MYSELF IS SO EASY,
BUT THE UN—BREAKING IS PAINFULLY HARD.

AS FOR LOVE, LET IT FLOW THROUGH ME
TO EVERYONE I SEE
AS I PASS BY

AS NOT TO STEP ON

ANYTHING OR ANYONE

ON THIS PLANET

EVER SO PAINFULLY.

SHE LEARNED TO LOVE HER ALONE TIME
WHEN SHE REALIZED HER OWN COMPANY
HELD SO MANY TREASURES ONCE
RESERVED FOR OTHERS.

SHE KNEW THAT
LOVE
(NO MATTER HOW BEAUTIFUL)

ALWAYS HURTS

AT THE END.

SHE UNDERSTANDS NOW
THAT GOLDEN CAGES ARE NOT DESIGNED FOR HER
(NO MATTER HOW SHINY).
SHE PREFERS DANCING BY A MOUNTAIN OR THE OCEAN
WHEREVER,
SHE CAN FEEL TRULY FREE.

SHE HAS IT ALL WITHIN HER.
TECHNICOLOR RAIN,
YELLOW BUTTERFLIES
& GOLDEN AUTUMN LEAVES.

YET, SHE KNOWS NOW
THAT WHEN HURRICANES COME

SHE CAN CHANNEL HER INNER THUNDER
AND THROW INTO IT
SOME GOLDEN,
GOLDEN SUNLIGHT

AND FEEL FINE WITH ALL OF IT.

SHE IS LIKE A VIBRANT FLOWER
GROWING IN THE DESERT,
UNEXPLAINABLY BRIGHTENED
BY LIFE'S JOY,

EVERMORE ALIVE AS
SHE FACES CHALLENGES.
AS A DANCER
SHE KNOWS TOO WELL
HOW TO DANCE.

—ADVERSITY

SHE KNOWS NOW
THAT AS LONG AS
SHE IS PRESENT
/LIKE NATURE/
IT WILL ALL UNFOLD
IN HER FAVOR,
WHICH IS NOW
TO BE
ALWAYS
HERE,
HEART OPEN,
VERSES FLOWING
IN HER ESSENCE.

SHE THOUGHT
SHE NEEDED
ONE PLACE
ONE HOME
TO FEEL SAFE
TO BE LOVED

UNTIL SHE DISCOVERED
THAT SHE CAN BE HAPPY
IN MANY PLACES,
DISCOVERING THE BEAUTY
OF THE WORLD
IN MANY HIDDEN CORNERS
FILLED WITH MAGIC.

IT IS NO LONGER NECESSARY
TO ESCAPE OR RUN AWAY
AS A FUGITIVE,

SHE WILL WALK AWAY
FROM ANYONE
FROM ANYTHING

THAT HARMS HER.

ONE CONSCIOUS STEP AT A TIME.

ONE SELF—LOVING THOUGHT AT A TIME.

ONE CONSCIOUS PRAYER AT A TIME.

SHE WILL CHOOSE HER WELL—BEING

CONSCIOUSLY,

AS MANY TIMES

AS NECESSARY.

DON JUAN,
CÚENTAME SOBRE EL CAMINO DEL CORAZÓN,
TELL ME ABOUT THE PATH OF THE HEART.

HOW DOES ONE GET TO IT?
DOES IT COME TO YOU OR MUST YOU LOOK FOR IT?

TELL ME MORE ABOUT IT.
MUST I BE PERFECT OR IMPECCABLE WHEN IT FINDS ME?

FREE OF SHAME AND REGRET?

OR

HOW DOES ONE BECOME WORTHY OF THIS PATH? — I ASKED HIM

I SEE YOU HAVE MANY QUESTIONS, SO FIRST, I WANT TO INVITE
YOU TO QUIET YOUR MIND A BIT.
I KNOW IT'S DIFFICULT IN TODAY'S WORLD. I HAVE BEEN THERE.
EL CAMINO DEL CORAZÓN WILL BECOME APPARENT TO YOU
ONLY AFTER YOU ENCOUNTER YOUR SHARE OF LOSS. GRIEF.
YOUR WORLD, AS YOU KNOW, WILL CRUMBLE. YOU WILL HAVE
TO GO THROUGH EACH STAGE OF GRIEF. FROM ANGER TO
ACCEPTANCE. TO ANGER AGAIN. TO VICTIMHOOD. TO... (SOONER
OR LATER) SURRENDER.

I KNOW IT SOUNDS QUITE ILLOGICAL THAT FOR ONE TO FINALLY ARRIVE AT THE JEWEL OF ONE'S HEART, ONE MUST GO THROUGH SO MUCH. BUT HUMANS, OH, WE HUMANS CAN BE SO STUBBORN, MOST OF US LOVING DISTRACTIONS AND EVERYTHING AND EVERYONE THAT TAKES US AWAY FROM THE TRUTH DE NUESTRO CORAZÓN.

I PROMISE I WILL CONTINUE TO TELL YOU MORE ABOUT EL CAMINO DEL CORAZÓN VERY SOON.

I MUST GO NOW, BUT PLEASE STAY WITH ME. YOU WILL FEEL SO LIBERATED ONCE YOU BEGIN TO TRULY LISTEN TO YOURSELF. — HE SAID.

113

SHE IS ENOUGH
WITHOUT HAVING TO BE
A RESCUER,
A VICTIM,
OR
A HEROINE.

SHE IS ENOUGH
JUST FOR BEING HERE.

SHE KNOWS,
    FALLING
        INTO

               HER BAD HABITS
IS SO EASY.

BUT

SHE IS BECOMING 

AWARE

ANYTIME

THOSE OLD ENERGIES
GRAB A HOLD OF HER.

SHE CAN SPOT THEM NOW,
CALL THEM BY THEIR NAME.

SELF—SABOTAGE

DOUBT

FEAR

AND LETTING THEM KNOW

CLEARLY:

I AM NO LONGER AFRAID OF

MY OWN BEAUTIFUL AND MAJESTIC LIGHT

✳ I AM NO LONGER AFRAID TO SHINE. ✳

ONE DAY,
SHE FORGOT ABOUT HER BIG DREAMS;
THE ONES SHE WAS PASSIONATE ABOUT
AS A YOUNG GIRL.

SHE BEGAN TO SEE THEM EACH DAY
A BIT MORE FAR AWAY AND
LOSING HOPE WAS NOT LIKE HER.

YET,
FROM TIME TO TIME,
SHE GETS A REMINDER,
A LITTLE SIGN TOO PERFECT
TO BE CALLED A COINCIDENCE.

AND

SHE BEGINS TO WONDER
WHAT IT WOULD BE LIKE
TO BE LIKE THAT YOUNG
AND HOPEFUL DREAMER AGAIN.

WHAT WOULD IT TAKE?
        FAITH — SHE SAYS TO HERSELF

AN IMAGINARY HOPE
FOR WHAT'S YET TO COME
STILL UNSEEN.

DIDN'T I DREAM IMPOSSIBLE DREAMS BEFORE?
I THINK I CAN DREAM THEM AGAIN.

SO

SHE BEGAN TO WRITE HER
MONUMENTAL DREAMS
IN SECRET,
AWAY FROM ANYONE'S EYES
AND SILENT WISHES.

"THERE IN THE SILENCE OF THE FULL MOON,
ONE DAY AFTER A MAGICAL SUNRISE
BATHED BY UNIVERSAL LOVE,
HER DREAMS WILL BE REBORN."

PERHAPS IT WAS TIME TO BELIEVE...

TRULY
    BELIEVE

        IN HERSELF AGAIN

YOU GET AWAY
TO CONNECT
AND YOU FIND YOURSELF
IN EVERY FLOWER
AND EVERY STEP
AS YOU CLIMB
AN UNKNOWN PATH
GUIDED BY A FRIEND,
AN ACCOMPLICE
WHO INVITES YOU
TO TREK A NEW WAY
INTO YOURSELF.

DEAR LOVED ONE,

HOW BEAUTIFUL IT IS TO SHARE YOUR LOVE FOR LIFE AND YOUR
SENSE OF WONDER WITH OTHERS.
THIS IS PART OF YOUR DHARMA.
REMEMBER TO STAY ON YOUR PATH AND TRUST THAT YOU ARE
ALWAYS BEING GUIDED BECAUSE YOU ARE.
KEEP LOVING EVERY PART OF YOURSELF; EVEN THE SHADOWS
OF WISDOM THAT LIVE WITHIN YOU SO YOU CAN KEEP LEARNING
TO LOVE OTHERS AS THEY ARE.

KEEP OPENING YOUR HEART AND WHATEVER YOUR NEXT STA-
TION IS... WILL EFFORTLESSLY FLOW INTO YOUR LIFE.

NOTHING TO PREPARE FOR,
NO EFFORT REQUIRED
BESIDES STAYING IN YOUR OWN LANE
OF HONESTY TO YOURSELF.

IT IS FINALLY YOUR TIME.
WHAT AN EXCITING SEASON THIS IS!

AND HOW I LOVE YOU FOR IT
FOR FINALLY ALLOWING YOURSELF TO BE HERE.

WITH LOVE,
YOUR HIGHEST SELF.

YOU WON'T COME
AND THAT'S FINE.

I AM HERE & THAT'S ALL I NEED
AND EVERYONE I LOVE IS HERE.

MYSELF AND MY TRUTH
WALKING FREELY IN THE AFTERNOON,

WAKING UP SIMPLY BUT FREELY.

THIS VERSION OF ME IS WHO
I HAVE BEEN WAITING FOR
ALL ALONG.

WHAT HEALS THE HEART:

- DEEP BELLY BREATHS
- WRITING BY HAND
- WALKS IN NATURE
- TRAVELING WITH CLOSE FRIENDS
- READING MAGICAL BOOKS
- SINGING OUT LOUD ANYWHERE (MY FAVORITE IS INSIDE MY CAR WINDOWS ROLLED DOWN, WIND ON MY FACE)
- COMMUNITY
- DANCING (HAVE YOU TRIED LATIN DANCE?)
- INTENTIONAL SILENCE
- HIGH VIBRATIONAL MUSIC
- CALMING AND CLEAN SPACES
- COLORFUL FRUITS AND VEGGIES
- FRESH WATER
- RESETTING YOUR NERVOUS SYSTEM (YOGA DOES WONDERS)
- SPEAKING YOUR TRUTH
- DISTANCING FROM ANYONE/ANYTHING THAT MAKES YOU FEEL LESS THAN YOUR RADIANT SELF
- CUDDLING WITH YOUR PET
- A GOOD CRY UNDER A COZY BLANKET
- THE MOON, THE SUN AND THE STARS

(MAKE YOUR OWN LIST)

LET ME DREAM:

THIS WORLD IS BEAUTIFUL

& REAL HUMANITY IS HERE

PEOPLE SPEAK OF LOVE,

NO HATE,

POWER & GREED BECOMES

LIGHTNESS OF BEING.

NO ONE GOES UNSHELTERED

NOR HUNGRY,

ORPHANS FIND THEIR LOST HOMES,

MENTAL HEALTH PATIENTS FIND GOD'S PEACE,

PRISONS BECOME SCHOOLS,

GUNS BECOME BOOKS.

LET ME KEEP DREAMING.

EVERYONE WE LOVE NEVER DEPARTS

&

THEIR SOULS FLY NEARBY.

EVERYTHING WE LOVE JUST TRANSFORMS & NEVER DIES,

INCLUDING

OUR SOULS.

THERE ARE PLACES THAT SPARK SOMETHING WITHIN US,
PERHAPS WHISPERING A LITTLE SECRET FROM OUR FUTURE INTO
OUR PRESENT.

YOU SEE A LITTLE MAGICAL CORNER AND IT SPEAKS TO YOU;
THERE IS A CALLING TO MOVE YOUR FINGERS THROUGH IT, TO
SAVOR IT AND YOU WONDER:

DID MY SOUL COME HERE BEFORE?

IT IS THE SAME WITH CERTAIN SOULS:
YOU SEE THEM & YOU ARE IMMEDIATELY DRAWN TO THEM AND
YOU CAN'T SIMPLY ESCAPE...

YOU JUST RISE
SIMPLY AND NATURALLY
IN LOVE.

GOD'S LOVE
ALL AROUND ME,
ABRAZÁNDOME.

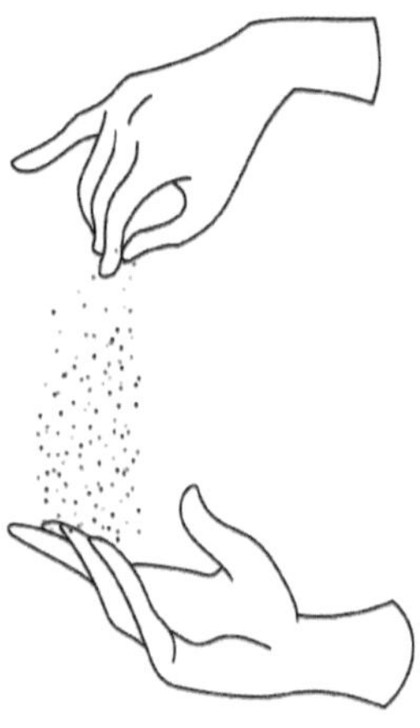

MAY YOU FEEL THE LOVE THAT WASHES OVER BILLIONS OF STARS
& EVERY LIVING BEING —INCLUDING YOU.

DON'T FORGET WHEN YOU SEE ME
THAT I AM NOT YOUR STRONGEST SISTER,
YOUR DEVOUT WIFE OR
DUTIFUL DAUGHTER,
THE SAVIOR NO ONE ASKED FOR
BUT VOLUNTEERED GLADLY.

WHEN YOU SEE ME
KNOW THAT I ALSO NEED
CANDLELIGHT AND
A DREAM OF PROLONGED
CALM &
LAUGHTER
WITH NO TRAGEDY COMING AFTER

SWEET RAIN
HONEST EMBRACES
&
LOVEMAKING

AN
UNEXPECTED RAINBOW
BEFORE A CALAMITY

ACCORDIONS BY MY WINDOW,
MEXICAN BALLADS,

LOVE SERVED AS A HEALTHY DINNER.

BECAUSE WHEN PEOPLE SEE ME
THEY MAY THINK
I DON'T NEED HELP

AND YET,
I WILL HAPPILY ACCEPT IT.

HALF OF MY LIFE,
I WAS A SURVIVOR.

THE OTHER HALF,
I BECAME
SOME SORT OF SAVIOR

NOW,
I AM FINALLY

A WOMAN RECLAIMING MY OWN HAPPINESS.

HOW BEAUTIFUL IT IS TO KNOW THAT BEHIND EVERY DIFFICULT
TIME IN OUR LIVES,

WHEN WE PERCEIVE OUR OBSTACLES AS OUR TRUTH,

WHEN WE ASSUME SCARCITY IS OUR REALITY OR EVEN WHEN
OUR HEART GETS BROKEN,

THERE IS JUST A NEW LIFE WAITING FOR US AROUND THE
CORNER,

WHERE GOODNESS COMES TO US EASILY,

WHERE ABUNDANCE BECOMES OUR HEAVENLY INHERITANCE,

AND LOVE TO ALL OUR ULTIMATE REALITY.

HURTING AND HEALING
AT THE SAME TIME
JUST GIVE ME SOME SPACE
TO UNDERSTAND
HOW CAN MY HEART STRIVE
TO FEEL ALIVE
WHEN IT FEELS
SO EMPTY INSIDE.
YOU MADE ME
WORK IT ON OVERDRIVE
AND NOW THAT
EVERYTHING SEEMS LIKE IT IS FINE,
AM I SUPPOSED TO SWITCH GEARS
JUST AS FAST...
WHEN MY HEART STILL HURTS
SO MUCH?

MY LOVE FOR YOU WILL NEVER CHANGE,
BUT PLEASE DON'T ASK ME TO BE THE SAME GIRL
YOU MET.

WHEN YOU AWAKEN: "EVERYONE & EVERYTHING BECOMES YOUR BELOVED."

ONE DAY YOU WAKE UP RENEWED
AS THE BRIGHTEST MIRACLE.

YOU MADE IT BACK AND I,
DO NOT KNOW HOW TO REACT.

I MEAN, ONE PART OF ME IS DEEPLY
HAPPY AND RELIEVED,
BUT IT HAS TAKEN ME A WHILE TO BELIEVE,

IS THIS EVEN REAL?

OR AM I DREAMING INSIDE A WORLD
WHERE EVERYONE I LOVE HAS FOUND THEIR OWN HOME?

THIS TIME AROUND,
IT FEELS PRETTY REAL.

WHEN I STARTED TO WRITE THESE PAGES
I DID NOT THINK YOU WOULD MAKE IT.

NOW AS I FINISH THEM:
YOU ARE ALIVE.
YES... YOU MADE IT.

I WOULD LOVE TO TELL YOU, MY BEAUTIFUL HEART, THAT YOU WILL NEVER BE BROKEN AGAIN,
BUT I WOULD BE LYING TO YOU AND I KNOW WE ARE BOTH DONE WITH LYING TO OURSELVES.

WE WILL HURT AGAIN AND MORE THAN WE WOULD LIKE TO, BUT THE GOOD NEWS IS THAT WE ARE NO LONGER AFRAID OF GOING DEEP AND HEALING AT OUR OWN PACE, CRYING THE DAYS AND THE NIGHTS AWAY UNTIL WE GET TO THE TRUTH OF EACH EXPERIENCE, SO WE CAN TRANSFORM IT INTO NEW GEMS OF WISDOM.

THE BEAUTIFUL THING ABOUT PAIN IS THAT IT MAKES US MORE COMPASSIONATE AND LOVING BEINGS AND CONNECTING WITH OTHERS THROUGH THIS KIND OF LOVING VULNERABILITY IS A GIFT.

SO, MY DEAR AND BEAUTIFUL HEART, YES.

WE WILL HURT AGAIN.

WE WILL CRY AGAIN.

WE WILL GRIEVE OVER LOSS AGAIN AND AGAIN.

BUT DON'T GROW WEARY BECAUSE YOU AND I ARE BEST FRIENDS NOW AND NOT STRANGERS. I WILL SIT IN SILENCE TO LISTEN TO YOU MORE OFTEN.

YOU SEE, MY BEAUTIFUL HEART, I FEARED YOU FOR SO LONG THAT I AVOIDED YOU IN EVERY POSSIBLE WAY BECAUSE I KNEW THAT IF I DUG DEEP ENOUGH, I WOULD FIND SO MUCH SADNESS STORED.

IT WAS SO MUCH EASIER TO LOOK THE OTHER WAY. SEEK ANY DISTRACTION, FILL MYSELF WITH TITLES AND ACCOMPLISHMENTS, WITH NEW THINGS OR DESTINATIONS, ANYTHING TO HIDE OUR SHADOWS.

YOU AND I KNOW THAT BECAUSE OF OUR JOYFUL NATURE, IT WAS SO MUCH EASIER TO HANG OUT NEXT TO OUR MOMENTS OF HAPPINESS AND CELEBRATION BECAUSE WE GENUINELY LOVE TO HAVE FUN!

DEEP DOWN, WE BOTH KNEW THAT KNOCKING ON THE HOUSE OF OUR SADNESS WOULD BE FAR FROM EASY AND WHY WOULD WE, IN OUR RIGHT MIND EVEN GO THERE?

EXCEPT WE DID NOT KNOW THAT
IT IS ALSO THERE THAT THE GOLDEN KEY
TO OUR OWN TRUE HAPPINESS LIVES.

THIS YEAR WAS THE ONE WE WENT DOWN THERE AND
EXAMINED IT ALL CLOSELY.
WE OPENED THE ATTIC OF OUR UNCONSCIOUS, OH, SO BRAVELY,
WE SWAM THE WATERS OF OUR CHILDHOOD AND MADE IT TO THE
SHORE.

IT WAS THERE, AFTER TAKING A FEW DEEP BREATHS THAT WE
COULD FINALLY SAY:
THANK YOU, LOSS.
THANK YOU, GRIEF.
THANK YOU, UNREQUITED LOVES AND UNLIVED DREAMS.
THANK YOU, LIFE, FOR EVERYTHING.

MY BEAUTIFUL HEART,
WE WILL BREAK AGAIN/ BUT MOST IMPORTANTLY/
WE WILL LOVE AGAIN /UNTIL THE VERY END/
FOR THANKS TO YOU/MY ONLY HOME/ MI CORAZÓN/
I CAN SAY I AM/ WHO I HAVE BECOME/

THANK YOU,
MY BEAUTIFUL HEART.

MY BEAUTIFUL HEART

YOU ARE WHOLE.
NO SCAR OR FRACTURE IS TOO DEEP
TO OVERSHADOW YOUR BEAUTY.

GOLDEN OCEANS FLOW
ALONGSIDE THE RIVER OF
YOUR VEINS AND YOU GLOW
MILES AWAY.

AND WHEN YOU ENTER A ROOM,
EVERYTHING LIGHTS UP WITH YOUR LOVING PRESENCE.

MY BEAUTIFUL HEART.
I KNOW YOU HAVE LOST PEOPLE AND
DREAMS, BUT THEY ARE NOT TRULY
GONE FOR THEY HAVE TRANSFORMED.

CLOSE YOUR EYES AND THINK ABOUT THEM.

TAKE YOUR DREAMS FOR INSTANCE,
THEY HAVE BECOME NEW DREAMS WITH BRIGHTER WINGS AND

AS FOR PEOPLE, THINK OF ANYONE WE'VE LOST AND VISUALIZE
WHO AND WHERE THEY ARE NOW:

THEY ARE ALL BETTER BECAUSE OF YOUR TIME TOGETHER.
THEY GAVE YOU SOMETHING.

YOU GAVE THEM ALL OF YOU AT THAT MOMENT.

MY BEAUTIFUL HEART.

YOU ARE WISE.

EVEN IF SOMETIMES, OUT OF FEAR
YOU'VE ACTED UNCONSCIOUSLY

FORGIVE YOURSELF.

YOU DID NOT KNOW ANY BETTER
AND WHAT ONE CALLS MISTAKES
ARE REALLY JUST THE NEXT STEP
INTO ONE'S HEALING.

MY BEAUTIFUL HEART,
YOU HAVE BEEN LOVED DEEPLY.

YOU HAVE KNOWN THE DEPTH OF LOVE
AND WHAT ELSE IS THERE TO KNOW...

SO,

I JUST WANT TO THANK YOU
MY BEAUTIFUL HEART,
FOR IT IS THROUGH YOU THAT I HAVE MET WITH GOD
WHEN IT WAS ALMOST TIME TO GIVE UP
(AND I AM GLAD WE DIDN'T).

WE'VE MOVED ON,
WE ARE HEALING...

WE ARE FREE(R).

THANK YOU

I AM SO GRATEFUL TO GOD, MY HIGHER POWER, THAT DIVINE ENERGY WITHIN — FOR GIFTING ME THIS NEW OPPORTUNITY TO EXPRESS MYSELF THROUGH THIS BEAUTIFUL ART FORM WE HAVE COME TO KNOW AS POETRY.

MIL GRACIAS TO ALL OF YOU FOR YOUR LOVE AND SUPPORT. I WANT TO THANK EACH PERSON WHO HAS INSPIRED ME DURING THIS SEASON DURING MY SOLO ADVENTURES, WHERE I FOUND DEEP SOLACE & REST WHEN I NEEDED IT THE MOST.

I FEEL DEEP GRATITUDE FOR MEXICO AND ITS BEAUTIFUL PEOPLE FOR EMBRACING AND HOLDING ME SO LOVINGLY DURING THIS WRITING PROCESS. FROM SAN MIGUEL DE ALLENDE AND THE WONDROUS WRITING RETREAT HOSTED BY MY DEAR FRIENDS ELI & JOSEPH TO THE RIVIERA MAYA AND ALL ITS ENCHANTMENT.

ALSO, I WANT TO GIVE THANKS TO MY BEAUTIFUL COMMUNITY AT ALEGRÍA PUBLISHING AND TO EVERY POET AND ARTIST THAT CONTINUES TO CHOOSE ME AS THEIR MENTOR ON THEIR CREATIVE PROJECTS. IT IS THE PRIVILEGE OF A LIFETIME TO BE ABLE TO SERVE A NEW GENERATION OF LATINE/X WRITERS AND POETS. YOU ARE MY MAESTRXS.

MIL GRACIAS TO THE BEAUTIFUL TEAM OF CREATIVES WHO'VE HELPED ME BRING THIS NEW POETRY COLLECTION TO LIFE:

CAMILA VILLOTA FOR HER VISUAL MASTERY AND CREATIVITY.

DIANE CASTAÑEDA FOR HER CREATIVE DIRECTION AND BOOK PRODUCTION.

CAMARI CARTER FOR HER HEARTWARMING FEEDBACK AND EDITING OF MY POEMS.

HIRAM SIMS, MY POETRY MENTOR IN LOS ANGELES. THANK YOU FOR REMINDING ME, I AM A POET.

AS FOR YOU MY DEAR READER, I AM INFINITELY GRATEFUL FOR LETTING ME COME INTO YOUR LIFE ONE POEM AT A TIME.

DAVINA FERREIRA IS A POET, SPEAKER AND ENTREPRENEUR, FOUNDER OF ALEGRÍA MEDIA & PUBLISHING @ALEGRIAPUBLISHING THAT CONNECTS THE WORLD WITH LATINX BOOKS & MAGAZINES.

FERREIRA WAS BORN IN MIAMI BUT GREW UP IN COLOMBIA. SHE IS THE QUINTESSENTIAL SYMBOL OF THE IMMIGRANT'S AMERICAN DREAM. UPON ARRIVING IN THE U.S. FERREIRA ATTENDED COLLEGE, RECEIVING A B.A. IN FINE ARTS FROM UC IRVINE AND WORKED AS AN ACTRESS AT WITH THE BILINGUAL FOUNDATION OF THE ARTS. LATER ON, SHE ATTENDED THE ROYAL ACADEMY OF DRAMATIC ART IN LONDON (RADA) TO PURSUE CLASSICAL ACTING. FERREIRA THEN COMPLETED A JOURNALISM CERTIFICATE AT UCLA EXTENSION AND BEGAN A CAREER IN JOURNALISM, WHICH LED HER TO LAUNCH ALEGRÍA MAGAZINE.

SHE HAS WRITTEN 7 BOOKS TO DATE, INCLUDING HER AWARD-WINNING POETRY COLLECTION, IF LOVE HAD A NAME, WINNER OF THE JUAN HERRERA POETRY AWARD BY THE LATINO BOOK FESTIVAL.

IN 2020, SHE RECEIVED THE CSQ MAGAZINE NEW GEN AWARD FOR ENTREPRENEURS UNDER 40 AT THE ROCKEFELLER CENTER IN NEW YORK CITY & OPRAH DAILY HIGHLIGHTED HER CONTRIBUTIONS TO THE BILINGUAL COMMUNITY THROUGH HER MOBILE BOOKSTORE.

SHE IS A SOUGHT-AFTER SPEAKER; WHOSE PASSION IS TO INSPIRE OTHER LATINAS TO SUCCEED AS ENTREPRENEURS AND TO EMBRACE THE POWER OF THEIR OWN STORY.

IN 2021, SHE PARTICIPATED AT HARVARD'S LATINA LEAD CONFERENCE & GOOGLE'S WOMEN'S SUMMIT.

IN HER FREE TIME, FERREIRA VOLUNTEERS BRINGING WELLNESS PROGRAMS THROUGH CREATIVE WRITING, YOGA AND MEDITATION FOR MENTAL HEALTH AWARENESS TO AT RISK YOUTH IN LOS ANGELES COUNTY THROUGH HER NON-PROFIT, ALEGRÍA MOBILE BOOKSTORES & ARTS COLLECTIVE.

EMAIL: DAVINA@ALEGRIAMAGAZINE.COM
INSTAGRAM: @DAVIFALEGRIA

www.ingramcontent.com/pod-product-compliance
Lightning Source LLC
Chambersburg PA
CBHW020044310726
48970CB00007B/2399